Text copyright © by Roberto Piumini 2001
Illustrations copyright © by Piet Grobler 2001
Originally published by Lemniscaat b.v. Rotterdam 2001
All rights reserved
Printed and bound in Belgium

CIP data is available

First U.S. edition

Doctor Me Di Cin

ROBERTO PIUMINI

Pictures by
PIET GROBLER

Front Street ⑧ Lemniscaat

Once there was a wise and famous doctor in China named Me Di Cin.

Me Di Cin was a very good doctor. His patients always recovered.

One day the emperor's son, Prince Ma La Di, fell ill. Refusing to play outside the palace, the prince had grown pale and thin. Doctor Me Di Cin was summoned.

"Prince, I think you need some fresh air!" said the doctor. "A walk in the countryside will do you good."

"Leave the palace?" the boy said. "I can't do that. I must stay here and work on my paintings. You'll have to cure me with herbs, as a doctor should."

"I'll see what I can do, Prince Ma La Di," said the doctor, and he went away. The next day he said, "Prince, I went to the hill

to look for herbs to cure you. But I saw only a laughing plant, a weeping plant, and a plant that waved at me."

"I have never heard of those plants," said the prince. "What do they look like?"

"Alas, I am a doctor, not a painter. Tomorrow I will search at the lake for a cure."

The next day the doctor returned. "I'm terribly sorry, Prince. I found jumping roses, singing nettles, and storytelling weeds, but I did not find the herbs that will cure you."

"How does the rose jump? What song does the nettle sing? What story does the weed tell?" the boy asked.

"Prince, I am a doctor, not a poet," Me Di Cin replied. "Tomorrow I will look along the river for the herbs."

The next day Ma La Di said, "I have drawn the plants you told me about, Doctor. Is this how they look?"

"Yes and no," the doctor said. "Plants change all the time. One day they look like this and the next day they look like that."

"But did you find the herbs to cure me?" the boy asked, a bit angry.
"I am terribly sorry, but I found only the lying mint, the timid

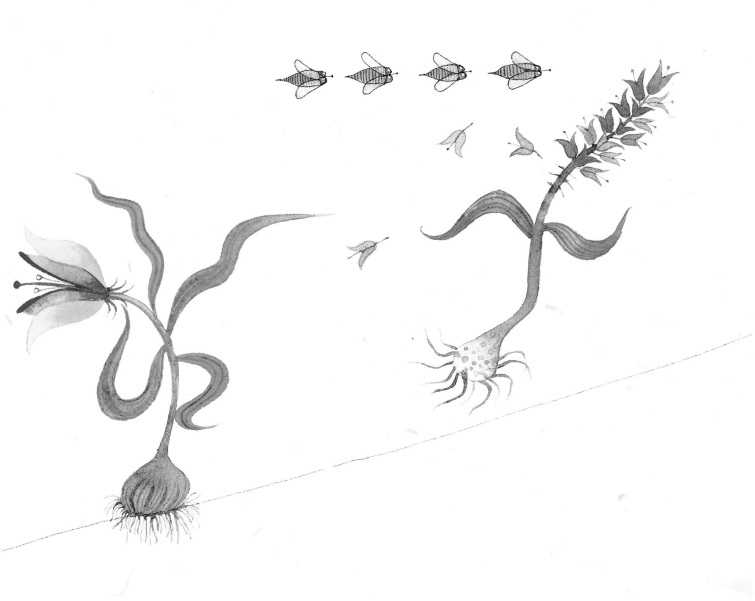

thyme, and the saving salvia," the doctor replied. "Tomorrow I'll go
to the valley to find the herbs that will cure you."

"Doctor, may I come with you tomorrow?"
the prince asked. The doctor bowed.

At dawn Doctor Me Di Cin and Prince Ma La Di went to the valley. They didn't find the herbs they were looking for, but

they saw lots of other plants — beautiful, ordinary plants. And
they saw jumping frogs, swimming fishes, and flying ducks.

The boy enjoyed it all so much that he was cured in a single day.

And every day after that, even when he became emperor, Ma La Di went for a walk with his old friend Doctor Me Di Cin.